Published by
Princeton Architectural Press
202 Warren Street
Hudson, New York 12534
www.papress.com

Text & illustrations © Marianne Dubuc, 2020
Original title: *Ours et le murmure du vent*
Published with the permission of Éditions Album Inc.
6520 Christophe-Colomb
Montréal, Québec H2S 2G8, Canada
All rights reserved

Translation rights arranged through the
VeroK Agency, Barcelona, Spain

English Edition © Princeton Architectural Press, 2022
Printed and bound in China
25 24 23 22   4 3 2 1 First English edition

ISBN 978-1-64896-119-9

This book was illustrated using pencil,
colored pencil, and watercolor.

For Princeton Architectural Press:
Editor: Stephanie Holstein
Typesetting: Paula Baver

Library of Congress Control Number: 2021939803

marianne dubuc

# BEAR AND THE WHISPER OF THE WIND

WITHDRAWN

Princeton Architectural Press · New York

Bear lived in a nice house.

Bear spent afternoons with good friends.

Bear sat in his favorite chair.

And he loved the smell of
freshly baked strawberry pie.

Bear lived a sweet life.

But that was before. One day, the wind changes, and Bear senses that it is time to go.

He still likes to sit in his favorite chair,
but it isn't as cozy as it used to be.
And he still loves the smell of strawberry pie,
but it doesn't taste as good as it used to.

With a rustle of leaves in the trees,
the wind gently whispers,
*"It's time for something new."*

So Bear packs his most treasured possessions
into his blue blanket and creates a bundle.

He leaves the door open as he sets off.
Maybe someone will make this their home,
Bear thinks.

Bear doesn't know where to go...

He only knows he
needs to go *there*.

Sometimes, Bear
feels very lonely.

And sometimes he feels as free as the wind!

One day, Bear comes to a clearing.
In its center is a cozy little house.

It's been so long since he's spoken to someone...
Bear has almost forgotten how.

Before Bear can make up
his mind, Rabbit peeks out
from a window.

"It's going to be dark soon!"
he says, inviting Bear inside.

Once Bear enters the cozy little house, he feels good—better than he's felt in days.

Bear gives his new friend a helping hand.

"There's been a strong wind and an old poplar has fallen on the roof," Rabbit explains.

"I have been lucky,
I could have lost my home!"

Bear understands.

To lose something, or someone,
that you love is very sad.

"Would you like a slice of strawberry pie?"
Rabbit asks.

Bear looks to the forest.
"No, thank you. I don't think I like
strawberry pie anymore."

Once again, he hears the whisper of the
wind telling him that it is time to go.

And so Bear continues his journey.

In his bundle he has added a tiny teacup,
a gift from Rabbit.

After walking for a few hours,
Bear is not sure of anything anymore.

He felt happy with Rabbit and wonders why he
couldn't stay in the cozy little house in the clearing.

A frog hops beside him to answer:
"It was not the end of your journey."

But Bear begins to worry, and he thinks,
Maybe I shouldn't have left MY home!
What if I have made a terrible mistake?

Now that he wants to go back,
Bear cannot find his way home.

I am LOST!!!

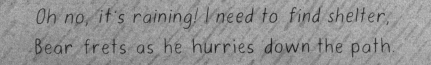

Oh no, it's raining! I need to find shelter,
Bear frets as he hurries down the path.

He finds shelter underneath a big pine tree.
"My bundle is full of water, and my boots are
like bathtubs!" Bear moans.

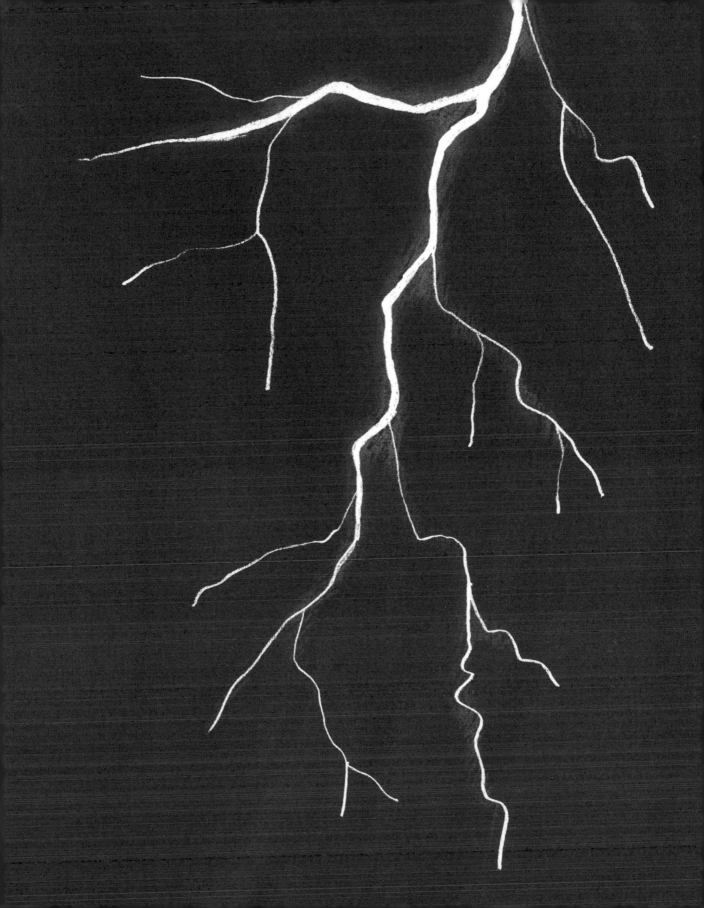

*I must not move.*

*I must hide under my pine tree.*

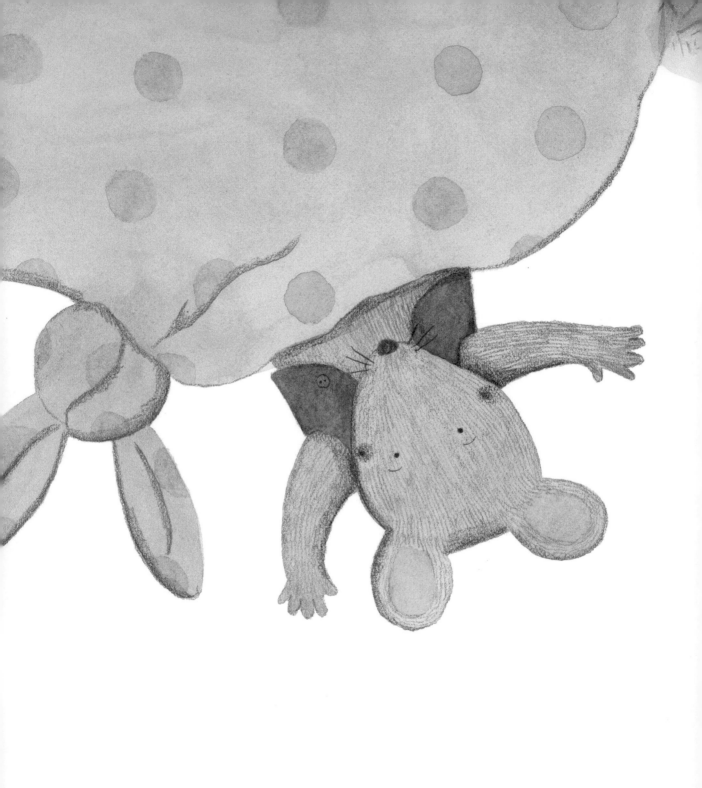

"Hello! Are you staying here for a long time?"

A funny little mouse is standing over him.
"My name is Mouse. Are you new in the valley?"

"I...I was hiding from the storm," Bear stammers.
Mouse smiles "The rain? But it's over!"

Bear discovers a little valley.

He loves the smell of the wet grass
and how warm the sun feels.

There is a stream.

There is a blueberry patch and his new friend, Mouse.

And though Bear can hear the rustling of the leaves in the trees, the wind is quiet again.

"Would you like a piece
of blueberry pie, Mouse?"

Bear now lives in a new house,
in his new favorite spot in the valley.

And his search has ended.